Pig in Love

First published 2005
Evans Brothers Limited
2A Portman Mansions
Chiltern St
London W1U 6NR

British Library Cataloguing in Publication Data

French, Vivian
         Pig in love. – (Zig zag)
         1. Children's stories – Pictorial works
         I. Title
         823.9'14 [J]

ISBN 0237529564
13-digit ISBN (from 1 January 2007) 9780237529567

Printed in China by WKT Company Ltd

Series Editor: Nick Turpin
Design: Robert Walster
Production: Jenny Mulvanny
Series Consultant: Gill Matthews

Pig in Love

by Vivian French

illustrated by Tim Archbold

Evans

When Pig fell in love
With Piggie next door
He took her red roses –

Then took her some more.

"I love you, dear Piggie!
I hope you love me!

Why don't we get married?
Please say you agree!"

But Piggie said, "No!"
And started to cry.

"My daddy won't let me
Until pigs can fly!"

Our Pig was a hero.
He made himself wings

Of leather and feathers
And tied them with strings.

He marched to the hill
At the top of the town,

But he couldn't fly up –

He could only fly down.

Then Cow floated by
In her spotty balloon,

21

"Hey, you there –
Come with me!
I'm off to the moon!"

23

"Oh YES!" shouted Pig
And his Piggie together,

25

"Let's fly to the moon!

And we'll stay there for ever!"

So Pig and his Piggie
Flew off and away...

Were they happy? You bet!
And they're happy today.

Why not try reading another ZigZag book?

Dinosaur Planet   ISBN: 0 237 52667 0
by David Orme and Fabiano Fiorin

Tall Tilly   ISBN: 0 237 52668 9
by Jillian Powell and Tim Archbold

Batty Betty's Spells   ISBN: 0 237 52669 7
by Hilary Robinson and Belinda Worsley

The Thirsty Moose   ISBN: 0 237 52666 2
by David Orme and Mike Gordon

The Clumsy Cow   ISBN: 0 237 52656 5
by Julia Moffatt and Lisa Williams

Open Wide!   ISBN: 0 237 52657 3
by Julia Moffatt and Anni Axworthy

Too Small   ISBN 0 237 52777 4
by Kay Woodward and Deborah van de Leijgraaf

I Wish I Was An Alien   ISBN 0 237 52776 6
by Vivian French and Lisa Williams

The Disappearing Cheese   ISBN 0 237 52775 8
by Paul Harrison and Ruth Rivers

Terry the Flying Turtle   ISBN 0 237 52774 X
by Anna Wilson and Mike Gordon

Pet To School Day   ISBN 0 237 52773 1
by Hilary Robinson and Tim Archbold

The Cat in the Coat   ISBN 0 237 52772 3
by Vivian French and Alison Bartlett

Pig in Love   ISBN 0 237 52950 5
by Vivian French and Tim Archbold

The Donkey That Was Too Fast   ISBN 0 237 52949 1
by David Orme and Ruth Rivers

The Yellow Balloon   ISBN 0 237 52948 3
by Helen Bird and Simona Dimitri

Hamish Finds Himself   ISBN 0 237 52947 5
by Jillian Powell and Belinda Worsley

Flying South   ISBN 0 237 52946 7
by Alan Durant and Kath Lucas

Croc by the Rock   ISBN 0 237 52945 9
by Hilary Robinson and Mike Gordon